Jake's Journal

by R. E. Kelley

For Audrey, Emma and Kathleen—who believed in Jake's story, and for my husband, Ivan, who helped me write it.

Published by Worthington Press
801 94th Avenue North, St. Petersburg, Florida 33702

Printed in the United States of America

2 4 6 8 10 9 7 5 3

ISBN 0-87406-675-1

Dear Jake,

Thank you for letting me use your journal for this book. I had to fix up some of the spelling and punctuation in the first part. But the judge is right about practice making perfect. In the last part I hardly had to change anything.

I couldn't think of a good title that wouldn't give away how it all comes out, so I'm calling the book "Jake's Journal" because that is what it is.

Thank you, Jake, for what you did for us this summer.

—D

Week One

I promised the judge I would start this journal tonight, so here goes.

The minute I walked in the courthouse I had a sinking feeling. Dark old wood. A weird smell. Nobody smiling. Petey was hanging onto Grandma so hard that she had to switch hands, so he must have felt the same way I did.

I don't like rooms without windows and the room they call the "judge's chambers" was awful. The judge was a real old guy with a gray beard. His shiny bald head was the only bright spot in the room.

He looked a long time at some papers he had that were about me. My report card and what the school counselor said, I guess. And the papers about the times I ran away and maybe the time I got into trouble about the candy bars I walked out of the store with.

Finally he said, "Now that your father is married and can provide a good home for you and Peter while your mother recovers, I'm going to give him custody for the summer."

The whole summer away from Michigan? In California with my dad? I hardly even recognized him when he showed up. I've never even seen his new wife. I wish Grandma had never called him when Mom took all those pills and got sick.

"Why can't we go stay at Grandma's?" I asked. "I'm already signed up for summer school. Grandma lives right by my school."

I'm not that crazy about going to summer school, but I thought it would make a good argument. I should have kept my mouth shut about summer school. That's what gave him the idea I should keep this journal.

"No," he said. "Your father loves you and wants to have you with him. Besides, you'll like California once you get there. I like it." He looked over his glasses at me. "It's different." So then he said he wanted me to keep this journal. He said writing in it would probably help me more than summer school. "It will help you think things through, Jacob. If you learn to write clearly, you'll learn to think clearly. Practice makes perfect."

He shuffled through his papers some

more. "I can see that you're not working up to your abilities." He pulled two big notebooks out of a drawer. "You'll be gone about two months. Here's one for each month. You don't have to write in them every day, but I want to see them full when you come back."

"You going to read them?"

"Not unless you want me to. But I want to be sure you fill them both."

He's a judge and I didn't want to get in any more trouble. Things are bad enough already, so I am going to do it.

I just read this whole thing over and I think the judge is crazy. How can I write clearly about things I can't even put into words? There are things that worry me so much I don't even want to think about them. The ambulance. Grandma crying as she flushed pills down the toilet. Dad and Grandma arguing all last night.

On the way home we stopped at the hospital to see Mom. She looked pretty good. She said she is going to live at a place called Recovery Haven for a while and we should have a good time in California and not worry, that everything will work out fine. But how can I not worry?

Saturday, June 20

Once the judge decided Dad could have custody, it didn't take him long to get us ready. We packed right away, then he drove us in his rental car to the airport in Chicago. He said we could get a better flight out of there than from Kalamazoo. So here I am up in a 747. I'm sitting by the window, but it's all clouds outside now, so I might as well write some more. The sooner I get these notebooks filled, the better.

At least now I have something good to write about. This airplane is all right, even if it was weird when we took off. I didn't hardly feel it when we started to move and things outside started going by. As we got going and began to climb, my stomach felt funny. I wondered if Petey's did too, and I told Dad we better not take any chances on him barfing. So Dad gave Petey some special kind of gum to chew and put him in the middle of us. But then, once the plane settled down, WOW! All the way from Chicago I could see practically the whole country below. There wasn't a single cloud. When we got to some mountains I took a chance on Petey. I let him sit on my lap for a while, so he could look out.

"See, Petey," I told him. "Those are mountains and desert down there."

"It looks like a sandbox," he said.

"Yes, but really it's a desert and great big high mountains."

"Maybe it's God's sandbox," Petey said. Then he turned around and said, quiet-like,

"Is Mommy going up to God, Jakey?"

"No, Petey, she's just got to be in a hospital for a while. She'll be all right by the time we come home again."

Dad leaned over us so he could look out the window, too. Petey didn't say any more. For only three, Petey is pretty smart. I know he wanted to stay at Grandma's, too. Our dad is okay, I guess, but I don't hardly know him any more. He's skinnier than he used to be and he's got real long legs. He always wears jeans now. Even when we were in the courthouse. He always wears boots, too.

I'll bet the judge could tell Grandma didn't like my dad, just by the way she looked at him. And every once in a while she'd look at his legs and kind of snort out of her nose. Just like my cat, Pussums, when a strange cat comes around. Maybe it's because Dad always wears jeans and boots. Grandma thinks even boys should wear ties and dress up.

I like the way he looks. And he always smells like the outdoors. In the courthouse and even here on the plane. When he leaned over us to look out the window he smelled real good. Not perfumey, like Mom. More like woods, and campfires, and fresh air after it rains.

I asked him how come he smells like that. He said, "I suppose because I'm outdoors most of the time, Jake. Why? Don't you like the way I smell?"

"It's okay. I was just wondering."

And that's not all I'm wondering about. I wonder what Dinah is like. That's Dad's new wife. If it wasn't for her, maybe the judge would have let us stay at Grandma's. I wonder if we really will get to go home at the end of the summer. I wonder why Petey asked me if Mom was going up to God. I wonder if Petey knows something I don't. Sometimes Petey knows things while I'm still only wondering.

I have to stop writing because we're getting ready to land. I sure wish it was Mom meeting us instead of Dinah.

This spending the whole summer with my dad is a big mistake. I can see already. He's okay but his wife, Dinah, sure has some weird ideas.

When she met us at the airport in Los Angeles, I could see right away she was funny. Funny-peculiar, Mom would say, not funny-haha. Mom is more funny-haha. She's always making jokes, except when she doesn't feel good. Not Dinah. She's funny-peculiar.

Her hair is in a thick braid, all wrapped around her head. It's not a wig or one of those things like Mom wears sometimes, either. It's all her own hair. After dinner she undid the braid. When she brushed it, her hair came all the way down her back in brown waves. She doesn't wear any makeup at all. Not even lipstick. Her eyes are so pale I had to look hard to see that they're kind of greenish. She's tall and skinny, too, like my dad. She even wears boots and jeans, just like him.

It's a good thing she's skinny, though, or she and I never would have fit into the tiny back seat of Dad's pickup. Me and Petey wanted to ride in the back.

"I'm sorry, no," Dinah said. "It's not safe if we have to make a quick stop. Here it's illegal even to let dogs ride in the back of pickups unless they're tied in."

Petey had to ride in the front seat where there was a shoulder strap. I had to squeeze in with Dinah for a whole hour. I wished I was back in Michigan, riding in Mom's big Buick.

Dad and Dinah live in Freel Canyon out in the Santa Juanita Valley. Their house is way down a dirt road. There are little bumps in the dirt, like waves. It kept us bouncing up and down. Mom's Buick is old, but it rides real smooth.

"You guys will get used to this road," Dad said when I complained. "We call it 'washboard'—like the old scrub boards people used before washing machines."

About then we went down into a wide dip with loose gravel all over it. "This part in here we call a 'wash,'" Dad said. "It's where the rains wash down off the mountains. When it rains hard, the wash fills up all the way across, just like a river. It's so deep I have to leave the truck on the other side and wade through the river to get to work."

He glanced sideways at Dinah and sighed. "Well, at least I won't have to worry about that if we have to move back to the city."

"How come you have to move?" I asked. Freel Canyon sure seems different from Michigan, but it's better than the bunched-together houses and apartment buildings we passed in Los Angeles.

"Our lease runs out in October." He pointed. "Hey, look!"

There was a big, yellowish-grayish snake in the road. "Get him, Dad," I yelled. "Run over him."

"No! Don't hit it!" Dinah said. "It's not

doing any harm. Besides it's only a gopher snake." So Dad stopped the truck until the snake got out of the way! "Look, Jake, isn't it pretty?" Dinah said.

Like I already wrote, Dinah's weird. A snake pretty?

Freel Canyon is really out in the sticks. Dinah said the only bus is the school bus. And that stops at the end of the canyon, down where the paved road ends. I hope nothing goes wrong so that I have to go to school here. I'd have to walk two and a half miles just to get to the school bus stop.

Unless Dad or Dinah take us somewhere, me and Petey are going to be stuck here for the summer. My dad doesn't even have a TV! Even the comics in the newspaper are all different. What am I supposed to do all summer, anyway?

Dad sounded real sad about having to move. He must like it here. But Freel Canyon is no place for kids—which is probably why there's hardly any kids. Dad told me about one, a guy named "Boomer." He lives about a mile further up the canyon. Dad said he'll start junior high in September, so he must be about my age, but a mile is a long ways. I wonder why they call him "Boomer." It sounds weird.

Sunday, June 21

It's so early in the morning that only me and Dinah's chickens are up. Mom always says, "Jake's my early bird. He gets up with the chickens." Now I know it's true. Mom is almost always right. Except just lately she's been kind of mixed up about things. Grandma said she'll get all better in Recovery Haven.

I woke up when Petey started talking in his sleep. He was jerking his arms around and crying out so loud he would have waked up Rip Van Winkle. Poor Petey is scared. He doesn't say much when he's awake, but I know. He's real worried about coming here to live. (And he's not the only one.)

When we got here yesterday, Petey was

practically hanging on my leg until Dad carried him up the stairs. What a lot of stairs! It's a strange kind of house, built right up a against a hill. First there's the garage. On top of that is a bedroom and bathroom and a little porch over the garage. And on top of that, on the third floor, is the regular house part. I never knew a house could have so many stairs just to get to the kitchen and living room. Dad said this kind of house is real normal in the canyon.

Outside, it's mostly brown hills and dead weeds around here, with mountains sticking up behind the hills. Right in front of the house, though, is the biggest tree I ever saw. It's so big four or five kids could hide behind it—if there <u>were</u> four or five kids here! Dad said me and Petey could have the downstairs bedroom, but the shade from that big tree makes it dark and gloomy. When Petey said he wanted to sleep upstairs with my dad, I didn't argue.

Dad said, "I thought you boys would like having your own downstairs apartment."

Petey shook his head. "I want to sleep up here with you."

From the look on his face I could tell Dad didn't like that idea. I thought he was going to say we couldn't. But Dinah spoke up. "That's all right. This first night it might be better for you boys to sleep up here." When it was time to go to bed, she fixed up the couch for Petey and pulled out a rollaway bed for me. I helped her put on sheets and blankets. The blankets smelled wonderful. Dinah said it's because she keeps them in a cedar chest.

'Course, they could have smelled like stinkweed and it wouldn't have kept me awake. It had only been dark a little while but Dad said it was almost midnight back in Michigan and Petey and I were still on Michigan time. I was so tired I fell asleep while the lights were still on.

It's a good thing I went to sleep right away like that. Later on in the night Petey woke me up and kept me awake off and on for a couple of hours. He kept crying, "Don't go, don't go!" Maybe he was dreaming of when Mom went to the hospital in the ambulance.

I sure hope that's what it was. I don't want anybody else to go away from us. And I don't want Mom to go up to God. It's kind of scary having a brother like Petey. Sometimes he seems to know about things ahead of time. I hope not this time!

Week Two

Yesterday morning Dinah called Boomer.
"Come on over for lunch, Boomer. But don't
bring Dutch."

"Dutch is Boomer's dog," she explained
after she hung up. "His folks half starve that
poor animal, so when Dutch gets loose he eats
anything he can catch, including my chickens.
He's got a mean look in his eye, too. I just
don't trust him and Boomer knows it."

It was about nine o'clock when she called
Boomer. Then she took me and Petey out to
the new chicken pen my dad built to keep

Dutch away from them. Seeing to the chickens is going to be what she calls our "morning chore." Dinah showed us how to give the chickens food and water. We helped her gather the eggs, too. She sells them to people who live down on the paved road.

By the time we got through, a scraggly-looking kid was coming up the driveway. Dinah looked at her watch. "Nine-thirty. A little early for lunch," she said. "Maybe Dutch isn't the only one over there who's hungry." Then she yelled, "We're over here, Boomer, by the chicken pen."

Boomer looked me up and down while Dinah told him who I was, and Petey, too. "Remember, Boomer," Dinah said, "Dutch can't come over here with you. And the same rule still applies—absolutely no killing."

"I know," Boomer said. "Not even stink bugs."

"And one more thing—no drinks from the hoses. You, too, Jake and Petey. Come inside if you want a drink."

"Same deal on horny toads and gopher snakes?" Boomer asked.

"Yep. I'd rather have them eating the bugs and varmints in my garden than have to control everything with poisons. Twenty-five cents for horny toads, a dollar for gopher snakes."

"You want to go hunting?" Boomer asked me.

I wasn't sure, but I said okay, anyway. He looked like a fun guy. His jeans had holes in the knees and his shirt had a rip in one sleeve and a dark stain down the front. His hair hung down over his ears and it was two colors. It was mostly brown, but the ends were light-colored. Just like when Mom used to get her hair frosted. He had a kind of sideways smile and I never saw such eyes as Boomer's. Seems like he looked everywhere

23

at once. His eyes might have scared me except for his smile.

Dinah packed a lunch for me and Boomer, with a banana and two ham sandwiches each. While she was handing them over, she said she wanted Petey to help her wash the eggs. That made Petey smile, proud-like. Grandma won't let him touch eggs on account of she thinks he'll break them. I wonder if Dinah told him she needed him to help her so we wouldn't have to take Petey with us. Mom is always making me let Petey tag along.

The first thing we did was hike up the canyon to Boomer's house. Dutch was outside, and before we even got up to the driveway, I could see that he was huge. Boomer said Dutch's mother was part collie and part German shepherd. He didn't know about the father. "Maybe a horse or an elephant," he joked.

When we got part of the way up the driveway Dutch started to growl. He lowered his head and the hair on the top of his back stood on end. I felt my body get all tensed up. Dutch wasn't on a leash or anything.

Boomer yelled, "Dutch, it's me." Dutch turned and crawled under the porch.

I didn't want to let on how scared I'd been. All I said was, "I'll bet there won't be any burglars at your house."

Boomer's folks both work for the movie studios, like Dad. Boomer says a lot of people who work for the studios live out here in the Santa Juanita Valley. There's an editor and a make-up man right down on the paved road.

Dad is a wrangler. He works with animals all day. Boomer said his folks are in "props," making scenery and stuff. When his folks are both working, Boomer is home by himself, so maybe it's a good thing he has that big dog.

My dad said studio work is "all or nothing." Dad either works long hours, day after day, or he doesn't work hardly at all. Boomer said it's the same with his folks. Sometimes they even work weekends.

Boomer told me I could get a drink from the hose by his barn. I took in a mouthful, but spit it out before I swallowed. Yuck! "What's wrong with this water? It stinks!" I said. "Is that why Dinah said not to drink out of the hoses?"

Boomer laughed at the face I was making. "Nah. All our water tastes like this. It has sulfur in it." Boomer took a big long drink, then wiped his mouth on his sleeve. "My dad says people pay good money to buy sulfur water. It's supposed to be good for you."

"Why does Dinah say not to drink out of hoses then?"

"That's just at your house." Boomer gave me a lopsided grin. "One morning when they were gone, I got a drink from one of your hoses. But I forgot to turn off the faucet. When Dinah and your dad got home that night the water tank on your hill was empty. Your dad told my dad that he didn't ever want me on the place again. But I guess now that you're here things are different."

Then Boomer said there was fresh spring water up the canyon. I decided to get a real drink then, even though the idea of drinking water coming out of the ground seemed strange. As it turned out, that wasn't the only thing strange up there at the spring.

Tuesday night, June 23

Petey woke up before I finished writing about the hike me and Boomer went on, so I'm finishing it now. The judge was right about one thing. California is sure different. Me and Boomer and Dutch climbed up past his house, way up a hill. In Michigan we'd call it a mountain but Boomer calls it a hill. We could see all the way down the canyon, past the wash, over to the freeway and all the housing tracts on the other side. There's a lot of people in California, but here in Freel

Canyon there's more trees than people.

It wasn't much of a hunt. We didn't see a single horny toad or snake, just rabbits and ground squirrels that Dutch tried to catch. And lizards—lots of lizards. Boomer said not to catch those because Dinah doesn't pay for them. Besides, he says they bite.

I glanced at Dutch. He was the only thing I worried about taking a bite out of me. But he seemed to be okay with Boomer around and after a while I forgot about him.

We ate lunch at the spring. The water was cold and tasted good after that yucky sulfur water at Boomer's. I could eat only one of my sandwiches, so Boomer took the other when he was done with his own. He gave half to Dutch. He told me he usually fixes himself cereal for breakfast and peanut butter and jelly for lunch. Even when Mom wasn't feeling good, she always got up to fix breakfast for me and Petey.

While Boomer was chomping on my sandwich he suddenly stood up and stared at the damp sand where the water from the spring spread out. "Wow!" he said. He pointed at a huge paw print. "That was some big dog!"

I looked. The print was wider than my hand, even bigger than Dutch's paw print.

Boomer put his face down close to it for a better look. Then he said a funny thing. "No toenails." He looked up. "The only tracks like that, that don't show toenails, is cats."

I figured he was putting me on. I could tell he thought I was a real city kid. Or maybe he just didn't see the marks of the toenails. 'Course Dad did say one time that there's bobcats around every now and then. I looked at the print some more. If this was from a bobcat, it would have to be an awful big one.

When we got back from the hike, Dinah said Grandma had called to say hello. Mom is okay, but she's not supposed to call us herself for a while. Dinah said it's probably part of the therapy.

Thursday, June 25

I had a terrible dream last night, so terrible I've been thinking about it all day. Maybe if I write it down it won't seem so scary.

I dreamed Dutch was chasing a rabbit, Boomer was chasing Dutch, and I was trying to catch up with Boomer. Dutch went head first over a cliff. Then I heard the most awful scream!

I woke up with a jerk and sat straight up in bed. Then I realized the scream part was real. It sounded like whatever made that hair-raising sound was right up on the hill behind our house. It was a warm night, but I was so scared I was shivering. I closed all the windows tight, hurried back to bed, and pulled the covers over my head.

This morning, Dinah said she and Dad hadn't heard a thing. But Petey must have heard it in his sleep, too. He woke up talking about a "bad thing" up in the mountains. He didn't know what it was, just that it was a "bad thing." I wonder if it was the same thing that made the big paw print by the spring.

When Boomer came over this morning, he said he hadn't heard the scream either. I couldn't even describe it for him, so maybe it was a dream. All the same, I was glad we decided not to hunt in the hills for horny toads and snakes today. Instead we went down the road to where Dinah made Dad stop to let the gopher snake get across. This time we took Petey.

We looked in the fields all along the wash. Boomer caught the first horny toad. Are they ever funny looking! All bumpy and scaly. They look like tiny dinosaurs with horns on their heads. When you catch them they get mad and squirt blood out of their eyes. I caught one, too, about as big as the palm of my hand, not counting the tail.

We stopped to eat. This time we had some tuna fish sandwiches, and while we were eating Petey whispered, "I see one." He pointed but I didn't see anything. "It's in that dirt," he said. "The dirt moved and I saw it."

"Catch it, then," Boomer said.

So Petey handed me his sandwich and clomped down on the dirt with both hands. Sure enough, he came up with a tiny horny toad, not much bigger than his thumb.

"Good for you, Petey," Boomer said. "Dinah will give you a quarter for it even if it _is_ little."

"I'm going to keep it," Petey said.

"Dinah won't let you. She says wild things aren't meant to be pets. Says that animals have rights, too. Sometimes she sounds like a preacher."

Petey looked like he was going to cry.

"Come on," I said. "We can ask her."

When we got home, Dinah gave me and Boomer each a quarter from her egg money. We let the big horny toads go in her garden. Dinah doesn't want to kill the bugs herself with sprays or powders, but if the horny toads keep the bugs away, that's nature's way, she says.

Boomer and me talked about that a little bit. He says Dinah is a "little loose in the flue." I guess he means weird.

"Thing is, if nature takes its way like Dinah says, there'll be so many coyotes here there won't be no place left for people," Boomer said. "And it seems to me there's more and more coyotes every year."

It sounded like Boomer was complaining about Dinah. I didn't say anything.

Well, when it came time for Petey to let his horny toad go, he cried. Dinah finally agreed to let him keep it two days. She said he would have to let it go after that. "But I've got another pet in mind for you, and it'll be used to you by the time you let the horny toad go," Dinah said.

"A kitten? A puppy?" I asked. I really miss Pussums. The last time Grandma called she said Pussums was fine. But I bet Grandma doesn't let her sleep on her bed like I did every night.

"No, not a kitten or a puppy," Dinah said. "We've had real bad luck with cats and dogs. The coyotes get them." Dinah sat Petey on her lap and looked at me. "Everybody likes to have something to hold, Jake. You and I have Petey to hold. And Petey's going to have a chicken to hold."

After dinner Dinah helped Petey pick out a chicken. She called it a "holding chicken." It's a little black banty hen with ruffled feathers. It didn't hardly even try to run away when Petey picked it up and put it in a box to sleep in. He named her "Bitsy."

Me and Petey sleep in the downstairs bedroom now, on the second floor above the garage. I used to think it was too dark and gloomy. But when it's hot in the afternoons, I'm glad we have a shady bedroom where it's cool.

Dad said he would put in air conditioning except he's just renting the place and will probably have to move out in the fall.

I asked him why he didn't just sign another lease instead of moving.

"It's a long story, Jake. Nothing we can do about it anyway," Dad said. "It's not your problem, son, so don't worry about it. You'll be back in Michigan by then."

I wish he wouldn't move. I'm beginning to really like this house. Petey doesn't mind sleeping downstairs any more, either. He usually falls asleep before I do. I don't think he sleeps too good, though. He thrashes around a lot. While I've been writing this, he stirred around in his sleep and mumbled something like, "I wish I could hold onto Dad. Not a chicken. Dad. I want to hold Dad."

"Are you dreaming, Petey?" I said. "Dad is too big to hold." I tried to laugh.

Petey went right off to sleep again, but I wonder. Sometimes Petey knows things! But it's silly to think Dad will go away just because Petey has bad dreams about it. Mom says everybody has bad dreams. I sure hope I don't have any more bad dreams like that scream last night!

Saturday, June 27

Turns out that maybe the scream was the wrong thing to worry about. Tonight, when I was in bed, almost asleep, I heard a rumbling noise, way off in the mountains. A wall creaked. The rumbling got louder and closer. Then the bed shook—hard! Something fell on my pillow, right next to my head. I grabbed Petey out of his bed. The whole house was groaning.

Dad shouted, "Jake!" I pulled Petey toward the door. Just as we got there, it opened. Dad grabbed up Petey and Dinah pulled me by the hand and we all raced downstairs. The rumbling stopped before we reached the ground, but the stairs felt shaky. I could hear things falling somewhere in the house.

Dad led us out away from the house and the tree, and a good way onto the driveway. Petey was crying for Mom.

"Here, let me take him," Dinah said. Dad passed Petey over and he quieted down. Dad put his arms around all of us as the rumbling and shaking started again. I would have been really scared, except for Dad and Dinah. The ground shook so hard I almost lost my balance.

"California's putting on quite a show for you, Jake. Feels like a humdinger to me," Dad said. "Must be a five."

"At least," Dinah said. "Maybe close to a six."

I never studied up on earthquakes, but I knew that the stronger they were, the bigger the number was. Six sounded big.

"Is the house going to fall down?" I asked. I'd seen pictures of houses that fell flat on the ground in an earthquake.

"Not unless it gets a lot worse than this," Dad said.

"This is a real old house, Jake," Dinah said. "It's been through quite a few earthquakes. Probably several stronger than this one."

"Think I'll see if I can get the truck out," Dad said. "We can listen to the radio, find out how close it was." He still had his truck keys in his pants pocket so he didn't have to go back upstairs.

The shakes were getting weaker and coming farther and farther apart, but I felt a lot safer when Dad backed the truck out and we all climbed in.

We listened to the radio and heard that the center of the earthquake was near the Santa Juanita Valley, which is where Freel Canyon is. After about half an hour without any shakes, Dad checked the gas and electric lines and then went in the house. In a few minutes he came back to the truck, carrying shoes for me and Petey.

"Looks okay," he said. "Books and dishes on the floor. Some broken glass. We won't be able to go barefoot for awhile."

"We'll get it all cleaned up tomorrow," Dinah said. "Now you boys had better get back to bed."

Petey had fallen asleep on Dinah's lap, but I wasn't sure I'd ever get to sleep again. "How about if me and Petey sleep upstairs by you?" I said to Dad. I felt a little babyish asking, but what if another earthquake came through? Besides, there was Petey to think about.

"Actually, it's probably safer on the second floor than on the third floor," Dad said. "But tell you what—suppose Dinah and I stay by you guys?"

So Dad lugged the rollaway down the stairs to our bedroom and he and Dinah slept on it. I didn't think I'd ever feel like going to sleep. I must have, though, because the next thing I knew it was pitch dark and Dad was grumbling, "Who the devil would be calling at four o'clock in the morning?"

I hadn't even heard the phone, and I went

right back to sleep. But in the morning over breakfast Dinah said it was Mom who called. "She'd just seen the morning news about the earthquake. She was so upset they gave her special permission to call to be sure you boys were all right. She'd forgotten about the time difference."

"Mom's a real worrier," I said.

"She thought maybe you should come back to Michigan to stay with your grandmother. But your dad said tornadoes do as much damage in Michigan as earthquakes do in California. Jake, do you want to go back to Michigan?"

I couldn't answer right away. Something happened when me and Petey and Dinah and Dad were all standing together while the earth shook under us. Now I feel like me and Petey really do belong with Dad, just as much as we belong with Mom. I finished my glass of milk and then I shook my head. "I guess we'll stay."

Dinah looked real happy. "Good. We'll have a nice summer together."

I hope she's right.

Week Three

Petey was right again—Dad is going away. Petey was dreaming about it last week, but Dad and Dinah didn't even know themselves until just last night.

Most nights when Dad comes home, even if me and Petey are in bed with the lights off, he stops in to check on us. Last night when I heard his truck, I was sitting up reading some comic books I borrowed from Boomer, so the light was on. But Dad didn't stop. He just kept right on going up to the top floor. I knew something was wrong.

I could hear Dad and Dinah talking. I couldn't hear what they said, but I could tell it was different from how they usually sound when Dad comes home.

After a while, Dinah came down and knocked on our door. (She always knocks. I wish Mom would.) "Jake, will you come upstairs? Your dad has to tell you something."

So that's how I found out that Petey's dreams were right, a whole week ago. Dad said, "I'm going on location in Arizona, Jake, right after the Fourth. I'll be gone for most of the summer. I can probably get home almost every weekend, but sometimes only for a few hours. I would like you to stay on here, son." He paused and looked at me.

"Do you have to?" I asked.

"Yes, just about. It's part of the business I'm in. That's why, before Dinah and I got married, I couldn't have you with me. I was on location a good part of the time. But I didn't expect to have to be gone this summer."

"How come you do then?"

"There's been a change in the filming schedule. But I want to be fair. I can call your grandma if you want to stay with her. Petey's too young to know what's best. You'll have to be the one to decide, Jake."

He got up and put his arm over my shoulders. "Dinah wants you to stay as much as I do. And I'll feel better if I don't have to leave her here alone. Think about it and tell me tomorrow night if I should call your grandma."

Well, I've been thinking all right. I love Grandma and I like to go to her house. But sometimes she gets excited about little things. Like when Petey's socks don't match, she makes a big fuss. Or if something gets spilled on the floor.

Dinah's different, all right. In weird ways but in nice ways, too. Petey broke a dish a couple of days ago and she didn't even yell at him. "We can always buy another dish," she said. One day Petey put on one red sock and one blue one. I wonder if he is color blind. Dinah just laughed and made up a little song about it.

"One sock is red,
   And one sock is blue.
   Diddle-diddle, Petey,
   I love you."

Then she tickled him to make him laugh and before long, I was laughing too.

Actually, most of the time Petey runs around here barefoot and in just his shorts. Grandma would <u>never</u> let Petey go outside like that, no matter how hot it was.

The only thing Dinah gets upset about is killing animals. Dad has a twenty-two rifle and last weekend he was talking about taking me out hunting rabbits.

Dinah had a fit. "You wouldn't, Slim!" she cried. That's the nickname she sometimes uses for Dad. "The rabbits and quail have as much right to be here as we do."

"Yes, and <u>we</u> won't have that right much

longer," Dad said. I was surprised at how sarcastic he sounded.

"That's right, throw it up to me," Dinah said.

I wondered what she meant by that. There must be something going on that I don't know about.

Dad said, "Well, honey, I just thought we could go back in the canyon and get a couple of rabbits for dinner. I'll cook them if you want me to."

"Are we so poor we can't buy meat?" she shouted at him.

Then they got into a big argument about the difference between buying meat at the store and shooting rabbits and eating them. When Dinah said she'd be glad to start serving vegetarian meals, Dad gave in. He promised we'd only shoot at targets. Darn it!

But other than that, I don't remember seeing Dinah yell or get upset. She's got weird ideas, all right, but she's easier to live with than Grandma. Dinah never tells us to shut up, or makes us go outside, or tells us to go watch TV—not that there is any TV to watch!

"If we stay will you take me target shooting when you're home weekends?" I asked Dad.

"Sure. And we'll have an extra good time this weekend," he said. "It's Fourth of July and there's going to be a parade. Do you want to go?"

"Sure. Can we have firecrackers?"

Dad shook his head. "I'm afraid not. They're not legal here."

"But who would catch us, way out here in the country?" I love cherry bombs. "How about sparklers? Petey loves those."

It didn't do any good. Dad said with all the dry brush and grass, even with sparklers there was too much danger of fire.

Boomer says his folks might bring him some firecrackers. I bet they don't. Except for a rope swing, Boomer hardly gets any stuff from his mom and dad. He even buys his own comic books out of the birthday and Christmas money he gets from his grandma and his aunt.

Petey is waking up from his nap now. I'll

46

have to tell him about Dad's plan to go to Arizona. I'll tell him we're going to stay here for the rest of the summer anyhow. I hope it all works out okay, with Dinah and everything. I just wish she wasn't so stubborn. And I wonder what she meant about "throwing it up to her" when Dad said something about not having the right to live here much longer.

Friday, July 3

An ant bit me this morning. I never saw such ants as they have here in Freel Canyon. They're great big red ones. This one got me right between my toes. The whole front of my foot is red. It hurts terrible, worse than a bee sting. Dinah gave me aspirin and a bowl of ice water to put my foot in. It still hurts.

If California ant bites are this bad I sure hope I don't get stung by a California bee. I haven't seen many bees, but there's lots of hornets. Weird Dinah won't let us kill them. She said the hornets kill the horn worms on her tomato plants. Grandma used to give me a dime for every horn worm I squished in her garden.

Dinah says it's nature's way for the hornets to kill the horn worms, but I'll bet she'd never let me kill them. Weird! She feels awful when people kill animals. I saw tears in her eyes yesterday. She was reading an article about baby seals being clubbed to death up in Canada, to make fur coats.

"It's not your fault, Dinah. You don't have a fur coat, do you?" I was pretty sure she didn't. I didn't tell her about Mom's.

"Heavens, no! No, I have to make my stand another way. I already have. That's why we're probably going to have to move in October."

"How come? Dad said it's a long story."

Dinah let out this big breath. "It's because I won't let the landlord hunt quail here any more."

"What happened?" I asked.

"The quail, hundreds of them, were around for several days last fall. Probably to get away from the hunters. At dusk, they'd all fly up into the oak tree at once. Just as though one of them had given a signal. They'd all be on the ground, then <u>whoosh</u>, and they were all hidden in the trees."

"But what about the landlord?"

"He showed up with his shotgun one morning. I saw him just in time. I ordered him off the property. 'Don't be foolish, woman,' he said. 'I've been hunting here for twenty years.' So I said, 'Well, you can't hunt here now.' 'But I own this property!' he said.

"I didn't know he was the landlord. I'd never seen him before. But I shouted right back, 'I don't care if you're the president of the United States. The way I look at it, those quail are my guests. You've got no business hunting them on this property while we're paying rent for it.'"

Dinah shrugged. "That did it! He looked me straight in the eyes for almost a minute. Then he said, 'If that's the way you want it, that's how it'll have to be, Miss.' I learned what he meant the next time your dad paid the rent. The landlord told him that an old Marine buddy, a hunting friend, is retiring soon. He's coming to California in the winter and the landlord's going to let him live here. So unless his hunting friend changes his mind, we'll have to move when the lease runs out in October."

So it's all Dinah's fault that they have to move. It doesn't make sense. Dad and Dinah have to move because Dinah won't allow any hunting here. But when they move, a man is going to move in who will probably hunt all the time. Then what'll happen to all the quail and rabbits and stuff Dinah's so crazy about?

Dinah says it's a "matter of principle." Sounds to me like what Grandma calls "biting off your nose to spite your face." The whole thing seems pretty stupid. I think maybe Dad thinks so, too.

He got home late last night, all pooped out. It was about all he could do to fish a cold drumstick out of the refrigerator for dinner. He told me how he and the other wranglers had to chase all over to catch some chickens they'd been using in the picture. He said it took longer to catch the chickens than it did to shoot the scene they were in.

"Do you ever use Dinah's chickens for the studios?" I asked.

"Nope. Most of hers are white. The studios don't use white chickens if they can help it."

"Why not?"

"Well, if they use brown chickens, most people don't notice if the chickens are in a different spot than they're supposed to be when a scene has to be shot again. But if they used white chickens, like Dinah's layers, people would notice them and remember. And every time they shot the scene they'd have to have a white chicken in the same spot. And believe me, chickens are not very cooperative. We had to catch twenty of the blasted things!"

Then he leaned over and whispered close to my ear, so Dinah wouldn't hear, "This is the way I like my chicken!" He shook the drumstick. Then louder he started talking about the Fourth of July.

"Are we going to the parade?" I asked.

"Yep. Better go early to get a good spot, too."

I like parades. So does Mom. I wish she could be here. The last time Grandma called she said Mom should be out of Recovery Haven soon. She's going to stay with Grandma for a while. I don't think I'll tell Grandma that Dad is going to Arizona. If she tells Mom, Mom will worry. She's a worrier. Maybe I inherited Mom's worrying just like Petey got what Mom calls her "intuition."

Week Four

The Fourth of July parade was great. There were four bands and so many horses I lost count. Dad knows a lot of the riders. When they rode past, they waved and yelled, "Howdy there, Slim," and stuff like that.

We had seats on the curb, but Petey got so excited he couldn't sit down. There was so much going on.

The Shriners were funny. They were a bunch of old guys on real little motor bikes. They rode in circles and weaved around and did tricks. Then a bunch of cowboys played like they were having a shoot-out and killing each other. Petey got scared, but Dad said they were only shooting blanks. There were Cub Scouts and Girl Scouts and Boy Scouts and Woodcraft Rangers, all in their uniforms. A group of kids in the 4-H Club rode by in a truck. Petey really liked the farmer overalls they were wearing.

After the parade we went to the park and ate hot dogs and cotton candy. I looked for Boomer but he wasn't there.

"Wouldn't you think Chuck and Ellen could make a <u>little</u> effort for that boy?" Dinah said.

"Not very likely," Dad said.

"Boomer said his dad might get him some firecrackers," I said.

"That sounds like Chuck," Dad said. "If Boomer starts shooting them off, you hightail it home, Jake."

"I wish we had room in the truck so we could take Boomer to see the fireworks show tonight," Dinah said.

"Me and Boomer could ride in the back," I said.

Dinah shook her head. "No kids in the back of pickups, thank you. If there's an accident you could flip right out."

"How about me?" Dad suggested.

Dinah didn't like that idea either, but Dad talked her into it just this one time. So after dinner, Dad put the mattress from the rollaway in the back of the pickup. Dinah drove and Dad stretched out on the mattress.

When we picked up Boomer he didn't look like Boomer at all. Not a single rip or stain on his clothes. He had even combed his hair. He climbed in the little back seat with me.

The fireworks show was at the park stadium. We got there before dark but the stands were already full. Guess everyone had the same good idea.

A western band was playing. Kids and grownups were dancing and running around on the field, waiting for the show to begin. People were laughing and having a good time. Finally it got dark and the fireworks started. WOW! There were rockets and stars and the sky was full of fire. Everything seemed like it was in silver and gold, and red and blue, and all kinds of different shapes.

"How do they make it go in patterns like that?" Boomer asked.

"I don't think I want to know," Dinah said. "It just seems like magic to me. It's good to have a little magic in our lives."

At first Petey was scared on account of the loud firecrackers, especially the ones that whistled. But after a while he liked it, too. As soon as we started home, he was so tired from all the excitement he went right to sleep. I almost did, too. The reason I didn't is on account of Boomer. He couldn't stop talking. I don't think he ever saw a fireworks show before. At least that's <u>one</u> thing I know more about than Boomer.

"Maybe you can come with us again next year," Dinah told him. I wonder if the "us" is

Dinah and Dad, or me and Petey, too. Does she think we're going to be here next Fourth of July? If Dinah and Dad move to a dinky apartment, I'd rather stay in Michigan with Mom.

After we dropped off Boomer and got home to our house, Dad carried Petey up the stairs to our bedroom. I got into my pajamas while he undressed Petey.

"I'll have to leave real early tomorrow, Jake," he said, tugging off Petey's shoes. "I might as well say good-bye now. It won't be until next Sunday—or maybe the Sunday after—that I get back." He blinked his eyes and looked like he was swallowing.

After he got Petey tucked in, he gave us both a kiss. "Good-bye, Jake."

"Good-bye, Dad."

He walked toward the door, then he turned back. "Thanks, Jake, for deciding to stay through the summer. This wasn't the way I planned things, but I can't turn down this job. It means extra money. We can all use it." He came back to the bed and shook my hand. "Take good care of Petey and Dinah for me, Jake."

My throat was kind of clogged up, so I just nodded. But as I was going to sleep I decided I'd rather have my dad than Boomer's. His dad acts like Boomer is just another dog, like Dutch. He even whistles for Boomer, just like when he whistles for Dutch. Even if I don't see much of Dad this summer, I know he loves me. I just wish he didn't have to be gone.

Saturday, July 11

Yesterday, me and Boomer tried to talk Dinah into letting us use the twenty-two for target shooting.

"Sorry, boys. Not unless your dad is with you, Jake," she said. "We don't want any accidents."

"We'll be careful," I said. "Dad showed me how to hold it. We wouldn't point it at anybody, even with the safety on."

"My dad lets me shoot his thirty-thirty," Boomer said. "Only there's something wrong with it. It's got to be fixed."

"Thank goodness for that," Dinah said. "You boys have no business with guns. There's a shooting accident in the papers almost every week."

So that was that. Dinah keeps the twenty-two locked away. Boomer said if he was me, he wouldn't be so chicken. He'd look for the key. I didn't tell him I already knew where it was.

He went home after lunch. It was so hot that Dinah made me and Petey stay inside for a while. Petey took a nap. I read some of Boomer's comic books. After Petey's nap we had ice cream and cookies. Dinah is weird but she's a real good cook. She even bakes all of our bread. She and Petey make the cookies from scratch. All kinds—with jam and nuts and raisins and oatmeal. When Petey and me went over to Boomer's to play in his sprinkler, she gave us some cookies to take to him.

I still can't drink Boomer's sulfur water. It smells like dead toads and rotten eggs. But it's cool and fun to run in. We can't do anything with the sprinkler at my dad's house. There isn't enough water. Everybody out here in Freel Canyon has water from wells. A lot of the wells have sulfur water. Dinah said the sulfur wells all have plenty of water. It's the wells with good-tasting water, like my dad's, that don't have much water in them.

Dinah said that's the only thing she doesn't like about summer in Freel Canyon, not having enough water. "But we're darn lucky to have this place, water or no water," she told me. "It's not easy to find a place in the country. I hope we don't wind up in an apartment."

I don't even want to think about it. What I really wish is that Dad and Dinah just stay put. Then they could put in a new well and get sulfur water to make a lawn and stuff. All the grass and weeds around here are brown and smell like dust. Dad and Dinah worry about fires all the time. The fires are like forest fires, but in southern California they call them brush fires, on account of there's no forests. Whenever we hear sirens Dinah runs outside to look for smoke.

Last Thursday we heard sirens and saw big gray clouds of smoke. It looked like the fire was right on the other side of the hill behind the house. Airplanes flew over us, close and awful loud. Dinah said they were carrying water to drop on the fire. I was kind of scared, but I tried not to let on. Petey was really scared on account of the loud noises from the planes. He always gets scared of loud noises. Sometimes I wonder if things sound louder to Petey than they do to everybody else.

Dinah held Petey on her lap and said we shouldn't worry. She said the firemen are just wonderful. "And besides, we can't smell the smoke. That means the winds aren't blowing the fire this way." All the same, she kept the radio on and every few minutes she'd look to be sure the wind hadn't shifted.

"It's because of the fires that your dad got so upset when Boomer emptied our water tank," Dinah said. "If a fire ever comes this way, we'll need that water to save the house."

"When did Boomer do it?"

"Just a few weeks before you got here. We've been trying to add a little extra water to the tank each day ever since. That's why we have to be so careful about showers and watering and never letting the water run. Now the tank is a little more than half full. Thank goodness!"

Me and Petey only get to take one quick shower a day. Dad calls them "miniature showers"—minute you're in, minute you're out. We can use all the water we want at Boomer's. But it sure stinks!

Grandma called today just after me and Petey got home from Boomer's. We talked about Mom and Petey and stuff like we always do. Then Grandma said, "How's your father?" It was the first time she'd even mentioned him— almost like now she might suspect something. (Maybe Mom gets her "intuition" from Grandma!)

"He's working a lot," I said, casual-like. It wasn't a lie. He is working a lot—in Arizona. "You want to talk to Dinah?"

So Grandma and Dinah talked a little while. Dinah didn't mention Dad being gone and working in Arizona this weekend, either.

Week Five

Dad had to work on Saturday so he didn't get home with the truck this weekend and Dinah couldn't drive it to deliver her eggs. So this morning me and Petey and Dinah walked five miles, all the way down to the paved road and back.

I wanted to ask Boomer to come with us, but Dinah said, "It won't hurt you boys not to see each other once in a while. Call him and tell him you'll be gone most of the morning. He can come over for lunch if he wants to, but not now."

Boomer sounded as though he was still in bed. "Yeah," he said when I told him we'd be gone. I could hear him yawning.

"She said if you want to come over for lunch you can, but you can't come now," I said. "I'll call you when it's okay for you to come over"

"Okay." It sounded like he banged the receiver down.

I helped Dinah carry the boxes of eggs and Petey carried a canteen of water. A little way past the big wash, we came to a huge oak tree. We sat down underneath to rest and have drinks from the canteen. Dinah said the tree was probably three hundred years old. Older than our country!

She pointed to a utility pole on the top of a hill nearby. "See anything different about that pole up there?"

I looked. "Nope."

"Count the wires," she said.

"There's three."

"Now count the insulators on the cross arm of the pole. How many of those do you see?"

I counted. "There's four. FOUR?" I squinted my eyes and looked again. "Hey! One of them's a bird, not an insulator."

"It's a red-tailed hawk," Dinah said. "I see him there a lot. He always perches on that cross arm very carefully. He's right where the fourth insulator would be—if there were a fourth insulator. He's in plain sight but perfectly camouflaged."

"What's he doing up there, anyhow?" I asked.

"He's hunting. From the top of the pole on the top of that hill he can see all around. He's waiting to catch something for breakfast, maybe a mouse or a kangaroo rat."

I don't understand Dinah. She and Dad

have to move because she won't let the landlord hunt quail by their house. She even takes <u>spiders</u> outside when she finds one in the house. But she thinks it's perfectly all right for hawks to eat mice and kangaroo rats. I asked her why.

"It's nature's way," she said. "If there weren't any hawks to eat the mice, there'd be too many mice."

Nature's way! If nature's way is so great, how come there are earthquakes and tornadoes?

When we got to the paved road, Dinah got the mail from the mailbox. She opened one of the envelopes and frowned.

"What's wrong?" I asked.

"Just a rent receipt and a note saying the landlord's friend is definitely coming and will need our house in October."

I didn't know what to say. The whole thing is so crazy! All for a "matter of principle"!

When we delivered the eggs, a lot of people weren't home. But Dinah knew where they hid their door keys. She could still get inside to leave the eggs in the refrigerator and pick up the egg money.

"Is that why you didn't want Boomer to come, on account of you didn't want him to know where the people hide their keys?" I asked.

"You figured that out pretty well," she said.

"Now me and Petey know."

"Yes. I trust you. And I know for sure that you and Petey won't be coming down here alone. Boomer might some day. He goes everywhere. Another thing is I know I can trust you to keep the hiding places a secret, not to tell anyone. I'm not so sure about Boomer." Dinah shook her head, kind of sadly. "Boomer's basically a good boy. But sometimes it seems like his folks just don't want to be bothered with him. He's too much on his own and I think it's why he gets in trouble sometimes."

It was a long five miles, that whole walk, especially after it got hot. I thought Petey would get tired, but he kept up with us pretty good without any whining. Seems like he's growing up faster here in California. He always used to run whining to Mom or Grandma when me and my friends wouldn't let him come someplace with us. But here, he mostly stays with Dinah when me and Boomer go off by ourselves. Dinah always tells him he's her special helper.

On the way back we stopped to rest again at the big oak tree. Petey passed around the canteen. He thought he was pretty important. "Thanks, Petey," I told him. "You want me to carry the canteen the rest of the way?"

"I can do it. It's my job," he said.

Dinah looked at her watch. "I hope Mr. Kreimer isn't home yet. He lives in the house back over there, in that clump of trees." She pointed to it. "He goes every morning to pick up the fruits and vegetables the supermarket throws away. He feeds them to his cows."

"Where's the cows? I want to see the cows," Petey said.

"You can't see them from here," Dinah

said. "They're on the other side of the house, behind the trees. They used to run loose all over the canyon, until Boomer's dad called the county. They made Mr. Kreimer keep the cows fenced in."

"Let's go see them," I said. "Petey likes cows."

"Not on your life," Dinah said. "Mr. Kreimer is the crabbiest man I know. We wouldn't even be sitting here except I know we're just outside his property line. The line goes right through the middle of this oak tree. Even so, if he sees us here he'll probably act like we're trespassers." She patted Petey's head. "Sorry, Petey, no cows."

When we got home I called Boomer. "I'm not coming over today," he said. "I got something for lunch here at my own house." He sounded mad, like maybe he got his feelings hurt when I told him he couldn't come with us. But when I asked if we could come over later in the afternoon to run through the sprinklers, he said, "Yeah, okay." I'm glad because it sure is hot today, 110 degrees!

Poor Petey. He had a bad accident yesterday when we went to play in Boomer's sprinklers. Boomer was still acting like he might be mad at me about the morning. At least he wasn't very friendly. So after I cooled off I went into his barn to look at some of his dad's cowboy stuff. Boomer and Petey stayed outside. They were taking turns on the rope swing and Boomer was giving Petey pushes.

I don't guess I was in that barn more than a minute when I heard Petey crying real loud. I ran out. Petey was sitting on the ground, holding his arm. "It hurts, Jakey. It hurts."

Petey's eyes were glassy-looking. He wouldn't let me touch his arm to look at it. "We have to take you home, Petey. Can you get up on my back?"

I squatted down and Boomer helped Petey climb on. Me and Boomer took turns carrying him home. It was a long mile. Dinah took one look at Petey's swollen arm and wrist and called Mrs. Morgan, one of the ladies she sells eggs to. She drove right over and took us to the hospital.

We spent <u>three hours</u> in the emergency room, and now Petey has a cast from his hand all the way up over his elbow. The doctor said he has to have a cast for six weeks, but if he's careful they can put on a shorter cast for the last three weeks. I hope I never have anything broken.

After Mrs. Morgan brought us home and Petey was feeling better, Dinah asked him questions, trying to find out how it happened. All Petey would say is, "I fell on it. I was on the swing. Then I fell off and broke my arm. Yeah. I <u>broke</u> it!" He said it like he was proud.

"I didn't even see it happen," I said. "I was in the barn." I didn't tell Dinah that Boomer was pushing Petey on the swing when it happened, and neither did Petey. I don't think Boomer would hurt Petey on purpose, even if he <u>was</u> kind of mad at us.

Petey tossed and turned all night. He was dreaming about snakes—or maybe it was the rope on the swing. I asked him this morning and it sounded like the rope and snakes were all mixed together in his dreams. Anyway, whatever he was seeing in his nightmare, he was thrashing around so much he kept banging his cast against the wall. I finally got up and pulled his bed away from the wall so I could get some sleep.

Wednesday, July 15

Me and Boomer went down by the wash this morning. Petey stayed home on account of his cast. I wish I'd stayed home, too. It got so hot I felt like the sun was cooking my skin. The winds were blowing hard, straight up the canyon, right at us. Boomer said, "It's a Santa Ana. Whenever hot dry winds blow in from the desert, that's what we call it."

"Is it going to be like this all day?"

"Sometimes it lasts for three or four days," he said.

We didn't stay in the wash very long on account of we were so hot. "I wish we'd brought a canteen," I said as we sat down under the oak tree on Mr. Kreimer's property line. "I've never been so hot and dry in my life."

"Let's climb up in the tree," he said. "Maybe it'll be cooler up there."

"Won't Mr. Kreimer be mad?"

"Nah. He's probably still down at the market getting stuff to feed his cows. He goes there every morning."

So we climbed up. Boomer was right. It was cooler up there in the leaves. But pretty soon Mr. Kreimer came home in his truck. It seemed like he came out of nowhere. At least I didn't see him right away, and it would've been just fine with me if I hadn't seen him at all. He was an old guy with a scraggly beard, and he looked mean.

"Get down out of there, Boomer," he yelled out his truck window. "I thought I told your folks to keep you home. And take your pal with you, whoever he is. Both of you—get out of my tree." Then he drove on up to his house.

"Dinah said the property line goes right through the tree," I said.

"If that's true, then the part that hangs over the road isn't Kreimer's," Boomer said. "Come on, we'll just move over to that big branch that's hanging over the road." So we did.

But pretty soon here comes old Kreimer on foot. With a shot gun!

"I told you kids to git! Now git the bejabbers out of there," he yelled. Then he shot the gun. Maybe he aimed over the tree. But some of the shot gun pellets went into the tree, above our heads, on account of leaves came down out of the tree, right on us.

We shinnied down that limb like lightning until we were close enough to the ground to jump. When we landed we took off running as fast as we could. That was pretty fast, what with the tailwinds from the Santa Ana.

"We better not tell Dinah," I said when we got to my driveway. I was panting like I've seen Dutch pant. "She already warned me about Mr. Kreimer."

"It's on account of my dad," Boomer panted back at me. "Kreimer used to let his cows run loose all over the canyon so he wouldn't have to feed them so much. They ate some of my dad's trees. Dad called the county on him. The county man made him fence the cows in."

Boomer bent over, trying to catch his breath. "Kreimer, he got real mad. He said if he had to keep his cows home, then my dad could darn well keep me home, too."

"He still shouldn't shoot at us with a gun," I said.

"Never mind. We'll fix him, the crazy old coot." Boomer sat down in the dirt and looked up at me with that sideways grin of his.

I plopped down beside him. "How?" I asked. It was about all I could get out, I was still breathing so hard.

"I'll tell you tomorrow." Boomer grinned again. "You just be ready early tomorrow when I come over."

"What are we going to do?"

"You'll find out. You just be ready. And be sure Petey don't come."

Boomer wouldn't say any more. I never know what to expect from Boomer, but it's kind of exciting. I hope we don't get in trouble. At least not in real bad trouble.

Friday, July 17

I wasn't even going to write down what happened at Mr. Kreimer's on account of somebody might read it. But now that Dinah knows I might as well.

Boomer showed up early yesterday morning like he said he would. I didn't have to worry about Petey wanting to come with us. He was helping Dinah make molasses cookies. Those are Petey's favorite. Mine, too. Dinah makes them soft and chewy, and they are the best-smelling cookies I ever smelled. They should make perfume like molasses cookies smell.

On account of the cookies, I would just as soon have stuck around. I wish I had. But Boomer kept after me. "Come on," he said. "Let's go hunting. My dad saw a gopher snake down by the wash on his way home last night." Then he winked when nobody else was looking.

I found out why he was winking when we

got down to the end of the driveway. Dutch was there, tied to a bush. Boomer untied him and reached into the bush. He pulled out a can of red spray paint. "We're going to fix old Kreimer. Come on, hurry up, before he comes back from the market," he said.

"What if he catches us? Or finds out it was us?"

"Quit worrying. Are you chicken or something? He'll never know!"

"Yeah, but what if he _does_ find out?"

"Listen, even if he thought it was us, he could never prove it. Anyhow, this paint washes off. My dad uses it at the studios."

When we got there we crawled up through the brush and looked to be sure Mr. Kreimer's truck was gone. Then Boomer ran to the barn. The big doors were both closed. In bright red paint, Boomer painted all across them "KREIMER IS KRAZY!"

We laughed and laughed. Boomer had a little trouble with the spray can and I laughed even harder when he turned around and I saw red paint all over his face.

As soon as he finished we hightailed it home to Boomer's house. "Where's Dutch?" I said when we got there.

"Oh, he's all right. He's probably chasing rabbits in the wash. He'll come home by himself."

Boomer changed his clothes. I helped him wash the red paint spots out. I didn't see any spots on me.

But that afternoon Dinah saw some on my pant leg and wanted to know what it was. I told her Boomer and I had been looking at some of his dad's paints. I was glad later that I didn't actually lie, because the truth came out.

When old Kreimer came home and saw his barn doors, he also saw Dutch in the field near the wash. That night he called Boomer's folks.

Boomer said his mom had just been bawling him out about putting sopping wet clothes in the clothes hamper. So when Mr. Kreimer called, she put two and two together and got the story out of Boomer. Boomer's mom must be like mine. Mom always finds out the truth sooner or later. Anyway, Boomer's mom called Dinah and told her everything. They agreed that me and Boomer would have to clean the paint off the barn doors.

"Your dad is supposed to be home tomorrow afternoon with the pickup. He can take you down there with buckets of soapy water and scrub brushes," Dinah said. "Maybe he can smooth things over a little with Mr. Kreimer, but it's probably too late for that."

This morning Dinah made me call Boomer early. "Tell him he can't come over at all today. It will do you both good. Give you a chance to think about what you did to Mr. Kreimer's barn."

As I was punching in Boomer's number on the phone, I heard her muttering, "As if we didn't have enough trouble with Kreimer already."

Boomer answered before I could ask her what she meant. I told him he couldn't come over today at all. Then Dinah said, "And you can tell him I'm grounding you until the end of next week."

So that's that! If he wants to, Boomer can come over here next week, but I can't go over there, or down in the wash. I can't go any place unless it's with Dinah.

"What's Dad going to say about all this?" I asked Dinah.

"I have no idea. But I know he's not going to like it."

"I guess he won't take me target shooting, either."

"Well, isn't that a pity," Dinah said. She can be real sarcastic sometimes. I don't know what's so awful about guns and target shooting.

I wonder if Dad will be real mad. I've never seen him really mad. I wonder what he'll do to me.

Week Six

Monday, July 20

Over the weekend Dad came home in a new Ford truck! It's got a big extra seat in the cab so we can all fit in easy—and Boomer, too.

Dad got in early Saturday morning before I was even dressed. Petey was eating cereal and I was trying to eat a piece of toast. I guess because I was so worried about having to tell Dad about the red paint, I didn't feel hungry. When he came in the kitchen and gave us all a hug, I felt like sinking under the table.

After a while, Dinah gave my shoulder a squeeze and said, "Jake's got something to tell you."

I blurted out the whole story.

"You what?" said Dad. He looked at me like he couldn't believe it. By the time I told it all again, I was crying.

He said, "Hold on now, Jake. There must be a reason. Why, son? Why did you do it?" He glanced over at Dinah and then back at me. "What have _you_ got against Mr. Kreimer?"

So then I told him about me and Boomer in the tree and Mr. Kreimer shooting over our heads.

"Why, that old fool!" Dinah said. "Why didn't you tell me that part, Jake?"

"On account of you told me about the tree being on Mr. Kreimer's property line. We shouldn't have climbed it."

"I don't care what you did," Dad said. "That old man had no business shooting a gun anywhere near you."

"That idiot!" Dinah said. She was so mad she was shaking. Dad likes his eggs sunny-side up, but she broke three yolks in a row, so he had to have them scrambled.

I started feeling hungry. The eggs looked

so good that Dinah fixed some for me and Petey. Dinah's chickens lay eggs with bright yellow yolks, almost orange. Petey says his holding chicken, Bitsy, lays the orangest ones of all. She should. He gives her all the good garbage scraps.

Dad was so disgusted with Mr. Kreimer that he forgot to be mad at me. And Dinah said to forget about being grounded. That afternoon Dad and Dinah and me and Petey and Boomer drove down to Mr. Kreimer's in the new Ford. Dad had sort of a smile on his face when he saw the barn door. "Too bad it wasn't where people could see it from the road," he said. I don't think he meant for me to hear that, but I did. Then he carried the buckets over. Dinah helped me and Boomer get started on cleaning the paint off while Dad talked to Mr. Kreimer.

At first old Kreimer yelled. He carried on about "varmints" when Dad complained about him shooting so close to us. Dad nodded but said me and Boomer were pretty <u>little</u> varmints, and he guessed

Mr. Kreimer dealt with a lot worse in the war. And Mr. Kreimer looked kind of sad all of a sudden and all he said was, "Yeah." He turned away quick. He put his shotgun down on the back steps and went in the house.

After we got the paint washed off, we all drove over to the car lot to pick up Dad's old truck. Now Dinah and me and Petey will have that one while Dad takes the big Ford to work. Dinah told Dad she wanted to do some shopping with me and Petey, so they decided Dad should take Boomer back home in the Ford so he could talk to Boomer's dad.

"I've been meaning to talk to Chuck about Kreimer, anyway," Dad said. "I know the old man had a really rough time in the war. But he's got no business shooting his gun over the boys' heads. No matter what they did." His lips tightened up just like when he and Grandma were talking to the judge. "Jed Kreimer is going over the edge, I'm afraid. He's dangerous. Chuck and I may have to do something."

"What _can_ you do?" Dinah asked.

"I don't know. Considering the other problems we have with Kreimer, it would be awkward for Chuck or me to bring charges."

I didn't know what Dad was talking about. I wanted to go with him and Boomer, so I could hear what our dads said.

But Dinah said, "No. I want you and Petey to come shopping with me." I was disgusted until I found out why.

The first store we went to was Hubie's Western Wear. "I got a check for a story I wrote," she said. "It was in the mail your dad picked up from the mailbox this morning. I know just what I'm going to do with it."

What a surprise! Dinah bought a pair of boots for Petey and a pair for me. Real leather, like the kind she and my dad wear. She even bought saddle soap and a special oil, so we can take care of them when we get back to Mom's house.

"But you have to promise me you'll wear them whenever you go out in the fields or the brush," she said. "Ellen and Chuck saw two rattlers on the road this week. If you see one, boys, just back away and it won't hurt you. It's when you don't see them that you have to worry. But at least the boots will help protect your feet and legs better than your sneakers."

Talking about snakes always worries Petey. He got a quivery look on his face.

"Now don't worry, Petey," Dinah said. "Just remember to keep your eyes open and watch where you're going. If you see a rattler, back away, that's all. Just back away." She took his hand. "Come on. You can help me pick out the peaches and plums at the market."

After we finished grocery shopping and came home, Dad already had a barbecue fire started. He'd bought fresh corn at a stand by the road. I made a salad with Dinah's tomatoes and Petey helped me set the table. With one hand, and being so short, he couldn't do much, but he tried. Dad cooked the best steaks and corn I ever had. He's a good cook, just like Dinah.

He's a good shot, too. Sunday morning, yesterday, he took me target shooting. It was okay, but not as great as I thought it would be. Maybe it'll be more fun if I get better at it. Dad says it takes lots of practice. "Squeeze it off," he kept saying. "Don't jerk the trigger." I got a <u>little</u> better at it.

I'm getting along a <u>lot</u> better with Dad. When Petey and me first came here, Dad seemed almost like a stranger. And I was really scared what would happen when he found out about the trouble with Mr. Kreimer. I like it here in Freel Canyon better, too. I wish it could work out that Dad and Dinah could stay here, but I don't guess there's anything I can do about that.

Week Seven

Tuesday, July 28

Boomer told me what our dads said about Mr. Kreimer. Boomer's dad said Mr. Kreimer is a crack shot with a house full of medals and trophies. He said Mr. Kreimer didn't used to be so crotchety before his wife died. My dad said maybe it's living by himself that makes him that way. They decided to wait until fall before they do anything. I can't figure out why that will make any difference.

Maybe I should ask Petey, ha ha. It happened again. On Saturday, while Dinah was fixing breakfast, Petey asked, "Can we have pancakes and sausage tomorrow, when Dad is here?"

Dinah shook her head. "He's not coming this weekend. He called last night to tell me."

"My dad likes pancakes and sausage. You fix them. I think he's going to come."

Dinah and I laughed at him. But sure enough, in the middle of the night, I heard the Ford pull into the garage. Petey was right again. It's spooky!

That Sunday, after pancakes and sausage, Dad took me target shooting for a while. I guess he felt bad that he had to leave so soon. He talked Dinah into letting me keep the rifle out for the rest of the day. Of course, I couldn't have any bullets, but Dad said I could clean the rifle after he was gone, and practice squeezing the trigger.

Dinah didn't like the idea much. "What about Boomer? What if he brings over some of Chuck's ammo?"

"Boomer's gone some place with his folks. He won't even be here today," I said. So she gave in and I got to keep the rifle out until bedtime.

After Dad left I cleaned the rifle just the way he showed me. Then I put it over my shoulder like you're supposed to carry them and went outside. Down by the front gate, I sat down under a choke cherry bush, pretending I was ambushing outlaws coming up the road. I saw a ground squirrel across the road and took aim. I had a good bead on him. I squeezed the trigger. That squirrel heard the click and disappeared into a clump of cactus. I was going to see if I could find his hole when I had a funny feeling I was being watched. I looked up, right and left, slowly, like an Indian scout. Nothing.

Then from right behind me I heard a grunt. I turned around. Not a foot away, peering through a choke cherry branch, was a face! Beard and all, it was old Mr. Kreimer crouched down behind me. I stopped breathing. I'm kind of surprised I ever started again, I was that shook up.

But he was sort of smiling as best I could tell with that beard. He said, low and kind of rumbling, "You had him dead to rights. What in the world you doing hunting varmints with an empty chamber?" He straightened up then. I kind of scrambled up, too.

I didn't know what to say. I was still mighty scared, but I remembered that old Kreimer was on <u>our</u> property this time. I said, "Dinah doesn't let me have any ammunition. She doesn't believe in killing, and besides, she said I'm not big enough to use a rifle by myself."

"That woman!" he said. "You're taller than that twenty-two, ain't you? Any gun you're taller than, you're big enough to use. Leastways that's how it was where I grew up."

"Not where Dinah grew up, I guess."

"She's got some mighty foolish notions. I got to give her credit, though. She sticks by what she believes, even if it <u>is</u> foolish."

"You sure move quiet, Mr. Kreimer. Were you a scout when you were in the war?"

"You might call it that. Say," he said, pointing his big hand back toward the house, "there's another squirrel. Put a round in the chamber next time, boy."

I looked and sure enough there was another squirrel running toward the big tree. But of course I didn't have any round to put in the chamber. And when I turned around the old man was gone. Like he had never been there. I suppose he was around the other side of the bushes. But I couldn't hear a thing. Not a footstep, not a leaf rustling, not a twig crackling.

I didn't tell Dinah. I think maybe she and Dad are wrong about Mr. Kreimer. When he shot over us so close, he knew just where he was aiming. He'd already told me and Boomer to get out of there. He was trying to teach us a good lesson.

He sure moves quiet. He could ambush anybody.

Week Eight

Tuesday, August 4

Not much going on until yesterday. Me and Boomer are working on a fort under the oak tree. We wanted to make a tree house, but Dinah was afraid the nails would hurt the tree. We told her lots of guys have tree houses. We should have saved our breath. Anyway, Dad has lots of old wood he said we could use for a fort as long as we keep the nails out of the driveway. When we get the fort finished we're going to paint it with Boomer's dad's paint.

Dad's wood pile is off to the side of the house. Yesterday we were poking around there, looking for the right boards to make a ladder. "Hold it!" Boomer hollered. "Listen!"

Then I heard something too, a sort of sizzling sound. Then we saw it—a rattlesnake! It was three feet long. Maybe more. It had a big flat head and it looked like trouble!

"We better go tell Dinah," I said.

"Nah. She'll just tell us to leave it alone. To get away."

"But what are we going to do?"

"I'll show you what we're going to do." Boomer picked up two rocks and handed them to me. He picked up two more for himself and threw them at the snake's head as hard as he could. "Come on. Don't be such a chicken."

So I threw mine, too. We kept throwing rocks until the head was all mashed in and we were sure it was dead. It was a mess and I felt kind of sick. I wished maybe we had just given it one good bash with a board, something that would have killed it faster so it didn't have to suffer any. I was glad when Boomer took a stick and moved it back under a bush where Dinah or Petey wouldn't see it. I didn't feel like looking at it any more, either. Maybe I wasn't chicken, but compared to Boomer, I guess I am still a tenderfoot.

Today Boomer brought a knife and cut off the rattles. There were nine. He has a set with twelve rattles at his house, but nine is pretty good. He stuck them in his pocket. We got a shovel from the garage and dug a hole. I reached over to throw the snake into the hole. "Be careful. Don't touch the head," Boomer said.

"Why not?"

"People can get killed by a dead rattler's fangs. They still got poison in them." I was careful all right, real careful.

We didn't tell Dinah, or Petey, either. Dinah would have been mad, and Petey already has enough nightmares about snakes. Last week when me and Boomer finally caught a gopher snake, Petey wouldn't come near it. Dinah wanted him to see how pretty and tame it was. She held it on her lap and tried to get Petey to touch it. He ran away, crying. Dinah gave me and Boomer a dollar from her egg money and we let it go down a gopher hole near her garden.

Poor Petey had another bad dream about snakes that same night. He woke up telling me a snake was going to get him. It worries me a little. He was right about Dad going away on location. Then he was right when Dad surprised us and came home in the middle of the night. Anyway, I'm glad Petey wasn't with us when me and Boomer found the rattler. And even though I wished we had done it another way, I'm glad we killed it, too, no matter what Dinah thinks. At least that's one rattler I know won't get Petey.

Wednesday, August 5

Today Dinah took Petey to the doctor to

get his cast changed to a short one. It doesn't seem like three weeks since he broke his arm. I thought this was going to be a long boring summer, but it's going fast.

Before she left, Dinah fixed sandwiches for me and Boomer. It was only morning, but already so hot out that we mostly just read books until lunch time. Dinah takes me and Petey to the library every week to get books. I always make sure to get a book about cowboys or bugs because Boomer likes those best.

After lunch me and Boomer walked up to his house. I used to think a mile was a long way. But when Boomer and I get to talking and looking for snakes and horny toads, it's not far at all. We messed around on his rope swing a while. Then we were running through the sprinkler when I heard Dutch bark. The next I heard was Petey screaming, "Jakey! Jakey!"

I looked around quick and there was Petey, and Dutch had a hold of him! We found out later Dinah had dropped Petey off at the end of Boomer's driveway. He was walking toward us when Dutch started snapping at his legs. It's a good thing he had on his boots. Petey turned to run away, but Dutch grabbed him by the seat of his pants and started shaking him. That's how Dutch kills rabbits and ground squirrels, by shaking them. I've seen him do it. And now he was trying to kill Petey!

We both started running and Boomer yelled at Dutch. But Dutch just kept shaking Petey. He didn't let go until we got there and Boomer grabbed Dutch by the collar and started hitting his nose while I kicked him as hard as I could.

When we finally got him loose from Dutch, Petey was trembling all over. I felt shaky myself when it was all over. I sat down on the ground and held Petey close on my lap while Boomer shut Dutch in the barn.

Then we took turns carrying Petey home. He cried the whole way. That time, it <u>was</u> a long mile.

When we told Dinah what happened, right

away she took Petey's overalls off. She looked him all over. It was like a miracle. There wasn't even a scratch.

"Thank God for the boots and overalls," Dinah said. Tears ran down her cheeks.

At first I didn't catch her meaning about the overalls. But then I noticed that Petey's pants were new and thick. Dinah explained that after the doctor had put on Petey's new short cast, she took him to Hubie's— on account of he'd been so good when they sawed off the old cast and put on a new one. Ever since Petey saw those kids in the 4-H Club wearing farmer overalls in the parade, he's been talking about overalls. He has a thing about them. When we go into town, if he sees a man in overalls he points and stares. The overall pages in one of Dinah's clothes catalogs are pretty near worn out from Petey looking at them.

So at Hubie's, Dinah bought him the best overalls they had. They are such heavy material and so stiff that when Dutch grabbed Petey, all he got was the overalls, not Petey's behind.

"We'll get you some more overalls tomorrow, Petey. And I'll mend these, too. Then you'll have two pairs." She held him on her lap and told me and Boomer to go in the kitchen. "Have some cookies if you want. But don't leave, Boomer. I want to talk to you."

Me and Boomer didn't feel like eating anything just then. From the kitchen we could hear Dinah rocking Petey and singing to him. Me and Boomer were real quiet. We could hear Petey kind of sniffling and trying to tell Dinah about Dutch coming after him.

"He shaked me, he shaked me," he kept saying. After a while he quieted down. (Maybe Mom should get a rocking chair.) Then pretty soon the rocking stopped. We looked and saw Dinah carry Petey into her bedroom. When she came out to the kitchen, Boomer kind of sank down in his chair.

"Boomer, how did it happen?" Her voice was quiet, too quiet. Like she was furious and just managing to hold it in.

Boomer sank lower in his chair. "I don't know. Maybe Petey threw rocks at Dutch or something," he said.

"Oh, come on, Boomer. Petey wouldn't throw rocks at Dutch," I told him. Petey loves all animals, except snakes .

"Even if he did, why would Dutch go after him?" Dinah said. "He <u>knows</u> Petey. Petey's been over there at your house lots of times."

"Yeah, but not lately," Boomer said. "Not since he had his arm in the cast and couldn't go in the sprinklers. Maybe Dutch forgot who he was. Or maybe Petey looked different in his new overalls and his arm in a cast. Maybe Dutch thought he was a stranger."

"I should never have dropped him off at your driveway." Dinah dabbed at her eyes with a napkin. "But Petey was so happy with his short cast, so proud of his new overalls. He wanted to show you boys right away, and I had milk and ice cream melting in the back of the truck. It didn't even occur to me that Dutch would go after a child, <u>a child he knew</u>. I should have known. I should have known." Then she started crying hard.

"Don't cry, Dinah," I said. "It wasn't your fault."

She blew her nose. "I suppose in a way it wasn't Dutch's fault, either. He's been taught to catch his own food and go after strangers. But a <u>child,</u> a little child he should have known?"

"Are you going to call the county?" Boomer asked. He sounded pretty worried.

Dinah had to wipe her eyes and blow her nose again before she could answer. "What good would that do? Even if the dog-catcher took Dutch to the pound, your folks would get another dog. A watchdog to keep off trespassers. Then they'd half starve it and make it into another mean cur, just like Dutch."

I could see Boomer didn't like what Dinah said about his folks and Dutch. Still, at least it didn't sound like she was going to make them get rid of Dutch.

"Dutch doesn't bother me," I said. I was still mad at Dutch, but I felt sorry for Boomer, too.

"So far! So far he hasn't bothered you, Jake!" Dinah said. "All the same, from now on you're not going over there while Dutch is loose. Petey is not to go there at all—not that I think he'll even want to. Before you go there, Jake, I want you to call Boomer first, every time. And Boomer, I want you to shut Dutch in the barn before Jake comes over. Is that clear?"

Boomer nodded.

"Don't just nod," Dinah said. "Tell me what you're going to do."

"I'm going to shut Dutch in the barn."

"When?"

"When Jake calls and says he's coming over to my house."

"Every time?"

"Yes, ma'am." Then Dinah wrote it all out and made Boomer read it and sign his name. I could see he didn't like that, but he signed, and then he sort of slunk out. I walked down the driveway with him.

"Petey didn't even get a scratch. He won't have to get rabies shots or nothing. Why's she making such a big thing of it? She's crazy, just like my dad says." Boomer kicked a rock so hard it rolled all the way down to the front gate.

All I said was, "Well, Petey did get awful scared." But I don't think Dinah's crazy at all, not about Dutch anyway. Once in a while he still growls even at me, so maybe she's been right about him all along. What if me and Boomer hadn't been there when he went after Petey?

Later I told her, "I'm glad you didn't call the dog-catcher. Except for his rope swing and the comic books he buys himself, Boomer doesn't have much else besides Dutch."

She nodded. "I know, Jake. And when you leave, Boomer's going to miss you a lot. His folks leave him alone so much. He'll need Dutch then."

Week Nine

Monday, August 10

Dad got in late Friday night. Me and Petey had a fan blowing all night in our room so I didn't hear him drive in or come up the stairs. For a few days last week it was so hot me and Petey wore just our underwear to bed. Just like it is in Michigan sometimes—but at least there's no mosquitoes!

It was too hot even for the coyotes. Almost every night we hear them yipping and yapping and yowling. Sometimes it's just one or two, sometimes whole bunches of them. They sit on top of the hills and mountains around our canyon and holler back and forth to each other.

But those hot nights last week we didn't hear the coyotes at all. Saturday morning, while we were all eating pancakes and sausage, I asked Dad, "How come we don't hear the coyotes when it's real hot at night?"

"Maybe it's been too hot for them to hunt at daybreak and dusk the way they usually do. Maybe they're quiet at night because they're busy hunting then," he said. "Nothing quieter than a coyote when it's hunting."

"Or sneakier," Dinah said. "I'll never forget the morning I lost one of my hens to a coyote. Practically under my very eyes."

Petey's face wrinkled up. "Will a coyote get Bitsy?"

"No," she said. "This happened before I kept the chickens shut up for the night. The hen and her chicks were out early. I saw them from the kitchen window. I had a piece of burned toast to throw out and was just taking it downstairs to the hen when I heard her give one squawk. By the time I reached the bottom of the stairs, only the baby chicks were there, running around peeping for their mother."

"The coyote came right in the yard?" I asked.

"He sure did. Grabbed that hen right from under my nose, almost." Dinah shook her head. "I never even saw him."

"Then how do you know for sure it was a coyote?"

"Oh, I <u>knew,</u> all right," said Dinah.

"You should've waited for him to come back and then shot him," I said.

Dad laughed. "That's easier said than done. I've never seen a coyote near our place to shoot. The only ones I've seen have been in the fields along the wash. Usually very early in the morning, when they head back up into the mountains for the day."

"Besides, Jake, the coyotes are doing what is natural for them to do," Dinah said. "No, I just fixed the chicken coop so I could shut them in safely for the night. And I don't let them out until it's broad daylight."

"Boomer said Dutch keeps the coyotes away from his house," I said. "Too bad a dog didn't work out for you. What kind was it?"

"It was a toy collie. And we had a kitten, too. But the coyote got the kitten, and it chewed up Sheppy so bad the vet had to put him to sleep," Dinah said.

Dad said, "I was so mad I put out a chunk of raw meat and stayed up two nights with the twenty-two, hoping that coyote would come back for the meat."

"Did you get him?"

"I never even <u>saw</u> him," Dad said. "I should have tried a white chicken. For some reason, coyotes seem to love white chickens best of all."

"Yeah, but what about the poor chicken!" Dinah said. "Coyotes like lambs, too. But it's a funny thing. Mrs. Crink, who raises sheep over in Willow Canyon, told me she sees a coyote out in her sheep pen nearly every morning. It comes in to get water and grain. Some mornings, she says, it's just lying out there with the ewes and lambs like it was a sheep dog."

"That is strange," Dad said. "Jed Kreimer had to give up raising sheep because of the coyotes. He told me he'd seen a coyote jump his five-foot field fence carrying a good-sized lamb in its mouth. They're not only smart, they're strong."

"I'd sure like to see one," I said.

"You might, if you get up early enough— say four o'clock—before the sun comes up. You could watch from the field by the wash. Not in Mr. Kreimer's field, but across the road from there."

Dinah started to argue with Dad about the idea right away, but Dad said it wasn't that big a deal. He said that even if I got lucky enough to see a coyote, it wouldn't stick around when it spotted me.

Boomer and I are going to try tomorrow morning.

Tuesday, August 11

Last night Boomer slept over on the rollaway. We set the alarm for four o'clock. It was still dark when we grabbed granola bars and bananas and took off. As we were crossing the field across the road from Mr. Kreimer's we found a bunch of white chicken feathers. Boomer said probably a coyote stole the chicken from Mr. Kreimer and brought it to the field to eat it.

We climbed up the little hill where the red-tailed hawk perches. The sun hadn't come up over the mountains yet, but from the early morning light we could see the field below. It sure was pretty. Everything looked so soft and quiet. When Dad and Dinah have to move I hope they don't move to the city.

From up on the hill we could see paths

through the weeds. Boomer said they were coyote and rabbit trails. We saw cottontails with their puffy white tails popping through the weeds. And big jackrabbits, too, with ears that looked as big as a donkey's. At first there were a lot of rabbits, but after a while they disappeared.

I was finishing my last bit of banana when Boomer grabbed my arm so hard I almost choked. He put a finger to his mouth and then pointed.

At first I didn't see anything. Then a movement through the brush caught my eye and I knew why the rabbits were all hiding. A coyote came loping up the trail that ran along beside the wash. He was heading toward the hills, just going along easy-like. He must have seen us or heard us or smelled us. Darned if he didn't stop and look right at us.

He didn't look scary or mean like I'd expected. He was a lot like a German shepherd, and not much smaller. He was shaped about the same and with the same brownish fur. He held his head high, with his ears cocked just like a dog does. Then he turned and loped away like he didn't give a darn whether we saw him or not.

All the way home Boomer was bragging about how he'd shoot that coyote if only he had his dad's thirty-thirty. He said as soon as his dad's gun gets fixed he's going to go down and shoot it. I don't think I would want to shoot a coyote that looks like a dog, only smarter and kind of more dignified. Maybe Dinah is right about some things.

While me and Boomer were sitting there on the hill waiting to see the coyote, Boomer told me about an airplane wreck he hiked up to see with his dad last year. It's up in the mountains, up the wash a long way.

Me and Boomer are going to hike up there and see it—if it ever cools off enough. Boomer said getting there and back would take almost all day. I wonder if we'll see any more big paw prints like we saw at the spring. I just hope we don't hear any terrible screams.

Week Ten

Not much to write about until just lately, when I've had a couple of bad scares.

The first scare came yesterday. I called Boomer to shut Dutch in the barn so I could come over. But Dutch was out in the hills hunting and Boomer couldn't find him. While me and Boomer were fooling around in the barn, Dutch must have come home and crawled back under the porch.

Boomer went in the house to get us ice cream bars. I decided to go inside, too. I started toward the back door. I heard a horrible growling. I looked over my shoulder. Dutch was behind me. The hair on his back was straight up. His jaw was open, baring his sharp pointed teeth. It gives me the shakes right now, just remembering those teeth coming at me.

I yelled bloody murder. Luckily, Boomer came right out and called him off. From now on, I'm going to wait until Boomer calls me back and tells me Dutch is in the barn before I go over. I don't know what's gotten into that dog, but he seems to be getting meaner all the time. Boomer will probably think I'm chicken, but Boomer never had a big animal like Dutch coming at him.

Anyway, I don't need to go to Boomer's. There's plenty to do at our house. Dad put up a basketball hoop. Me and Boomer shoot baskets almost every day. Petey tries, too, but it's too hard for him. Dad got him another ball, one he can bounce. He plays with it in the garage on account of it bounces better on the cement.

That's what he was doing this morning when I had the second bad scare. I was shooting baskets by myself. Boomer hadn't come over yet. I wasn't paying much attention to Petey in the garage until I heard a horrible squawk.

Petey was in the back corner of the garage, staring at something. I ran over to see what was wrong. It was a <u>rattlesnake!</u> Littler than the one me and Boomer killed, but he meant business. His tail was shaking, making a sizzling sound like bacon frying.

His head was lifted up, pointing at Petey's bare ankles. I could hear Petey saying real low, almost like moaning, "I can't back away. I can't back away."

He couldn't. He was trapped in the back corner of the garage, with no way to get past the rattler.

"Stay still, Petey, real still," I said, trying to sound calm—which I wasn't! I ran into the house and took the stairs two at a time, yelling, "Get the twenty-two! A rattler's after Petey!"

Dinah was already grabbing the key from behind the clock when I got upstairs. "Where is it?" She unlocked the cabinet and loaded the gun.

"In the garage." Like a flash, she was down the stairs and into the garage, and I was right behind her.

"Shoot it! Shoot it!" I yelled.

"Quiet, Jake. I can't shoot it."

I couldn't believe it. There was Petey trapped by a rattlesnake and still she wouldn't shoot it.

"Are you crazy?" I said. "It's going to kill Petey. If you won't shoot it, I will!" I reached for the gun.

"We can't shoot it," she said quietly. "The bullet might ricochet and hit one of us." She bit her lip and whispered, so Petey wouldn't hear, "If I miss, the snake will strike for sure. Petey's too close to it." Then she handed me the gun. "Here, take this. But don't use it!"

She grabbed the hoe that she uses in her garden and held it up over her shoulder. Keeping her eye on the snake the whole time, she started moving sideways, real slow.

"I'm coming, Petey," she said. "That's a good boy. It's going to be all right, honey." Then she edged a little closer, circling around the snake toward Petey, just a few inches at a time. "Take it easy, honey. Stand real still. That's it."

By the time she worked her way past the other back corner, the snake had turned his head toward her a little. She inched toward Petey another foot or so. The snake slowly turned his head to watch her until he was looking straight at her.

WHOP! She chopped off his head with one whack of the hoe. Dinah is skinny but she's a lot stronger than she looks.

"Mama, Mama," Petey cried and ran to her. She picked him up and we all looked at the snake together. It kept wiggling something awful. Boomer says they don't stop wiggling until sundown.

Petey's face was covered with tears and so was Dinah's. "Come on, boys, let's get out of here. I can't bear to look at it," she said.

"On account of you killed it?" I asked.

"Well, partly, I suppose. It wasn't the snake's fault. Nobody told it to stay out of our cool garage on a hot day. Or to watch out for a little boy and his bouncing ball." Then she started crying real hard. "But mainly . . . I can't bear to look at it . . . because . . . because of . . . what might have happened to Petey."

Dinah carried Petey all the way up the stairs to the top floor and I carried the twenty-two. After I took the ammo clip out I called Boomer.

When he got here we all went down to the garage. "Can I have the rattles?" he asked.

Dinah looked at me.

"I don't care. I don't want them," I told him.

He had his knife with him. There were seven rattles. After he cut them off he started to put them in his pocket.

Petey said, "I want them!"

"You sure?" Boomer asked. He knew how scared Petey had been of the gopher snake that we'd caught, wouldn't even touch it. And I'd told him about Petey's nightmares about snakes.

"Yeah," Petey said. "I want to show them to my dad." So now the rattles are on Petey's night stand, right next to his pillow. When he put them there, I thought they would give him more bad dreams.

"I thought you were scared of snakes," I said.

"I am a-scared of them," he said. "But now I know my mama will save me. Now I won't have any more bad dreams about snakes."

It was the second time he called Dinah

"Mama," so I guess that's how Petey sees her now. He figures he has a "Mommy" back at our regular house and a "Mama" out here in California. It sounds funny to hear him call Dinah "Mama," but I guess it's okay with me. And I'll bet he won't have any more nightmares about snakes.

Mom—our real mom—called for the first time since the earthquake. She said she's at Grandma's now and can call us as much as she wants. Darned if she didn't want to talk to Petey first. So, of course, he blabbed the whole story about the rattler. That started her off, worrying about something that was already over and done with. She worries too much.

The last thing she said was, "Jake, take care. I worry about you. I can hardly wait for all three of us to be together again. Please, Jake, be careful. Don't let anything happen." Why is she worrying about me so much, I wonder.

Week Eleven

Thursday, August 27

The second notebook of my journal is full, so Dinah gave me this yellow pad to finish up on. I have to stay off my feet for a few days so I have a lot of time to write. And there is a lot to write about.

Me and Boomer had been talking about hiking up to see that plane wreck for a long time, ever since he told me about it. But when I asked, Dinah said, "You'd better not, Jake. Maybe next summer you can hike up there with your dad."

"Next summer I might not even be here. Next summer <u>you</u> probably won't even be here."

Dinah looked so sad I was sorry I'd said it. "Well, ask your dad then."

When I asked him last weekend, he thought for a long time. Finally, he said, "I think it's okay. Boomer knows his way around this canyon and up the mountains as well as most grown-ups." Then he winked at me. "You're not a tenderfoot any more, either."

"We'll be careful," I promised.

Later, when Boomer came over, Dad got out his Forest Service map. He put an "X" on it where the plane wreck is. "It's at the end of Rabbit Canyon. Follow the wash up past Mr. Kreimer's until it forks. Take the left fork up Rabbit Canyon and keep climbing. You can't miss it. But it's quite a hike to get there."

"Yeah, I know," Boomer said. "My dad took me and Dutch up there last year."

"You can forget about taking Dutch this time. You know how Dinah and I feel about him," said Dad.

Boomer didn't say anything about that, and I didn't either. But I was secretly glad Dad was making sure Dutch wasn't going. I'd just about had enough of that dog.

"One more thing," said Dad. "The springs are probably all dried up by now. You'll want to bring a canteen of water for yourselves."

That was last Saturday. On Monday it finally cooled off, with a nice breeze. The weatherman on the radio said it was going to stay on the cool side, so we decided to go the next day. Dinah still didn't like the idea, but she helped us pack a lunch and snacks. Early Tuesday morning we loaded up backpacks. We wore T-shirts, but Dinah made us tie long-sleeved shirts around our waists. "Just in case," she said.

Boomer and me cut across the field on this side of the wash, instead of going all the way down the road. When we got to the wash we saw Mr. Kreimer just going out in his truck. Boomer stuck out his tongue, but Mr. Kreimer was too far away to see. I waved. I couldn't be sure, but it looked like he waved back.

Everything went fine in the beginning. We saw lots of quail. And jillions of jackrabbits and cottontails. No wonder they call it Rabbit Canyon. But the wreck was farther than it looked on the map. The farther up the canyon we went, the harder it got to climb. We had to push through thick brush and climb some steep rocky slopes. We were glad we had the long-sleeved shirts. We put them on to keep from getting scratched.

We'd planned to eat lunch at the plane wreck, but we didn't make it that far before we got hungry. After lunch, when we finally did get to the plane, there wasn't much to see. It was all smashed up. A lot of stuff was gone, even the wings and the engine. We poked around for a while, but all that was left was rusty and busted. Somebody must have hauled the big heavy engine out somehow. Maybe it's flying around today. I wondered if anyone got killed in the crash, but Boomer didn't know.

We didn't stay long. "We're never going to make it home by supper," Boomer said. "When I came up with my dad there was a better trail, probably from a lot of other people coming up to see the wreck. All those rock slides we climbed up are new, too. From the big rains last winter, or from the earthquake."

"Do you think we'll get home before dark?" I asked.

"Yeah, if we hurry."

If I learned one thing about hiking that day, it was not to hurry down a rock slide. We were about a third of the way back down the canyon, just past where we'd eaten lunch, when we came to a jumble of rocks we had to get down. As I hurried after Boomer, my foot slipped. I fell and started to roll.

The next thing I knew, and it must have been a lot later, I looked up and saw a cliff over me. I'd rolled down the rock slide and right on over the cliff. I guess I must've passed out. The sun was already down behind the hills. I shivered. The breeze was chilly. My right leg hurt bad, <u>real</u> bad. I tried to move it and passed out again.

When I came to it was almost dark and the breeze was gone. The sky was purple, like it gets just before the sun disappears. My leg still hurt like crazy and I was afraid to move it, afraid I'd get unconscious again. I figured Boomer must have gone for help. But could anyone find me in the dark? I listened hard, hoping to hear people coming.

It seemed like forever, but then I heard a faint rustle. Something was out there, but I didn't know what. I couldn't hear it or see it—but I knew it was there, getting closer. I tried to move and nearly passed out again. My right hand touched a rock. I grabbed it.

I held onto that rock like I never held onto anything before, and I waited. I felt like yelling "help" but there was nobody to hear me.

Then I saw it! Yellow eyes in the dark. Just a few feet away! The biggest cat I ever saw. The cat I'd heard scream in the night, and it was coming toward me! I wanted to scream, but nothing came out. It got closer.

No sound. That mountain lion moved like it was floating on air. I never even saw its feet move but it came closer and closer. I swear I could smell its breath in the still air and see its white fangs in the fading light.

I kept my arm back, ready to throw the rock as hard as I could, right at those fangs. I was scared all right, but mad, too. I think I was a little out of my head. I whispered low, almost growling, "Those are pretty tough teeth, but I'm going to break some of them before you get me for dinner."

He leaped!

In the same split second I heard a WHAM! WHOOSH! Seemed like the cat changed course in mid-air and disappeared in the brush. Then instead of yellow eyes it was old Jed Kreimer's whiskery face bending over me.

"You can tell your daddy I shot pretty close to you again, boy," he said. Then darned if he didn't wink. He stripped off his shirt and wrapped it around me. "Feeling a little shaky there?" he asked. "We'll get you fixed up."

Me, I couldn't say a thing. It was crazy. All I could think of was how white Mr. Kreimer's T-shirt looked next to his wrinkled dark skin. The next thing I knew he was taking the T-shirt off and bending over my leg. "You've lost a bit of blood from that knee. That's a nasty cut, son. Could be broke, too. Never you mind, I'll get you out of here."

He cut the sleeves of his T-shirt into strips. I wanted to ask why, but I was limp as a wet paper towel, too weak to even thank him for saving me from the mountain lion. I watched as he cut a few branches. He wrapped up my knee with the T-shirt first. Then he put the branches around my leg and tied them with the strips from the sleeves to make a splint.

He hid his gun back under a bush. Then somehow he packed me up on his back and we headed out. He was breathing real hard the whole way, but I never thought an old guy could be so strong. Every so often he stopped to rest, but all the same, we were almost down to the fork in the wash by the time the rescuers and Dinah showed up.

Lucky for me, Mr. Kreimer had been out hunting the coyote that's been stealing his chickens. He saw Boomer running home all by himself. It worried him. He'd seen us both go up the wash in the morning. He'd recognized me when I waved. He figured something was wrong and came looking for me.

When Boomer got to our house, Dinah

called the Sheriff's Office and they called the Mountain Rescue Team.

The Mountain Rescue men gave Mr. Kreimer back his shirt. They wrapped me in a blanket and put me on a stretcher. When I told them about the mountain lion and how far Mr. Kreimer had carried me on his back, they made a big fuss over him. The sheriff's deputies and the men from the Mountain Rescue Team all shook his hand and patted his back. Dinah cried and threw her arms around him.

"Now, Missy, now now," he kept saying. "You just get on to the doctor's with him and get that leg put right. He's a brave one. Was going to fight that puma with a rock. A brave young one like that—we won't want him to lose his leg. You get along now, Missy." I think he was embarrassed to have people fuss over him.

Boomer had been standing there listening. When Mr. Kreimer told about me and the rock and the mountain lion, his mouth dropped open. I bet he won't ever call me chicken again. It turned out my leg wasn't broken. I had to have surgery to tie things together inside, and a lot of stitches. But it's going to be all right, except for a dandy scar, the doctor said. He taped it up, with an aluminum brace so I can't bend it. It makes it hard to get around.

But I'm not complaining. I'm real lucky. First Mr. Kreimer saved me from the mountain lion. And my leg isn't broken, either.

My gosh, there's somebody knocking at the door. Who could it be?

Thursday, August 27
Later

Now I think the whole thing might have been a <u>lucky</u> accident, on account of what happened this morning.

I was resting on the couch, writing, when there was a knock on the door. Mr. Kreimer had come all the way up both sets of stairs without me or Dinah or Petey hearing him. I don't know how he does it. When he knocked, Dinah rattled the dishes she was putting away and Petey knocked over his blocks.

Dinah offered him some coffee and cookies. "Thank you kindly," he said. "Just came by to tell you what I found out when I went back to collect my gun. I tracked that puma for a good three miles and only saw a couple drops of blood. Must be I only creased him."

"You didn't kill him then?" Dinah asked.

"I meant to. Could be I aimed a mite high, worrying about hitting the boy, and shooting from above."

"Thanks. It was close enough!" I remembered those yellow eyes and white fangs coming at me and the whoosh of the bullet past my head.

"I suppose sooner or later you'll get him," Dinah said.

"Not me, Missy. If that old cat keeps hanging around, we'll have a lot less trouble with the coyotes. If a coyote is scared of anything, it's a puma."

"Won't the puma steal your chickens, too?" I asked.

"Naw. They don't come that close to the house. Too wild, unless they're mighty desperate. Even if he does, that cat wouldn't do near the damage a bunch of coyotes would. He probably covers a fifty-mile territory. There's a lot of wild game for him up there without having to come down here with humans." He grinned. "'Course, he'll be passing through here once in a while, so don't fall off any more cliffs!"

When he stood up to leave, Mr. Kreimer said, "Thank you kindly, Missy. Those are might good molasses cookies."

They were, too. Dinah made them fresh for me early this morning because they're my favorites. She put some in a sack for Mr. Kreimer. Much as I like them, I wouldn't have cared if she'd given them <u>all</u> to him.

He turned to me. "One thing, though, son. If I was you, I'd take that twenty-two next time I went up in the hills. And be sure to take some ammo with you, too!"

"I'll see to it," Dinah said. What a surprise!

"One more thing," he said, winking at me. "Aim a little low if you're shooting from above. Maybe when you're back here next summer, you and me can get in a little practice back up there in the canyon."

"Thanks, Mr. Kreimer, but I probably won't be here. My Dad and Dinah have to move in October."

"I think you can forget about them moving, son." He said it to me, but he looked at Dinah. I didn't know what he meant, but Dinah did.

"Are you saying what I think you're saying, Jed?" she asked.

"Yep. Have Slim drop by any time you want to open an escrow on the place. I'm sure we can agree on a price. You've got a fine, brave boy there. Be proud to have his family as neighbors." Then he winked at me again and went out the door.

I could hardly believe it—Jed Kreimer is the landlord Dinah had the fight with! And he's going to let Dad and Dinah stay and buy the place. Dinah was so tickled she called Dad as soon as Mr. Kreimer went out the door. She called person-to-person and didn't even wait until nighttime when it's cheaper.

Later, when she was fixing dinner, me and

Dinah talked about killing and nature's way and stuff. We've both changed our ideas this summer. Boomer laughs at me, but Dinah's got me taking spiders outside. They're real funny looking if you take a good look at them. The black and white ones are cute, kind of pretty.

Dinah says she realizes now that sometimes killing animals can be necessary. After all, she killed the rattlesnake that was after Petey herself. "If Jed Kreimer had killed the mountain lion, I wouldn't have been mad or sorry. The important thing was to save you, Jake. That's part of nature's way, too—for a mother to protect her young. To put the safety of her young above all else. This summer I'm your surrogate mother."

I'm not exactly sure what the word meant, but I got the idea it had something to do with being a stand-in mother. So I said, "You're our summer mother, Dinah. I hope you can be our mother next summer, too."

Dinah said she hoped so, too. She said it was like a miracle. They are going to get to stay— because of me! Because Mr. Kreimer likes me.

It's a good thing I didn't know Mr. Kreimer was the landlord, though, or I would never have kind of made friends with him down by the road that time. And if I hadn't talked to him then, I wouldn't have waved at him when me and Boomer were going up to see the plane wreck. If Mr. Kreimer hadn't noticed me waving and known to come looking for me when he saw Boomer running home alone, I wouldn't even be here to be writing this!

Mom is all better now and me and Petey are going home next week. After I show this journal to the judge, I'm going to mail it back to Dinah. She says she might make it into a book. Wouldn't that be something!

About the Author

R. E. Kelley's first story for children was published in *Ranger Rick* magazine. The International Reading Association selected it as the best published short story for children in 1985, and she has been writing for children ever since.

The author—whose full name is Ruth E. Kelley—grew up in a small village near Buffalo, New York. Although she never had a dog or cat for a pet, in the summer she caught frogs and tadpoles and crabs in Murder Creek, which ran through her backyard. Sometimes she dangled her hand in the creek so the minnows would nibble at her fingers.

But in the wintertime, in snowy upstate New York, she read and read and read.

After she graduated from the University of Michigan, she and her husband moved to southern California where they lived in big cities. Later, after their daughter and son were born, they moved to an old house in a rural canyon north of Los Angeles. Besides the wild squirrels, rabbits, birds, gophers, kangaroo rats, and snakes, the Kelleys' pasture has been home to sheep, cows, burros, a horse and ponies, pigs, Shetland sheep dogs, Pomeranians, and too many cats to keep track of.

Mrs. Kelley still likes to read, especially about people who seem real. So when she wrote *Jake's Journal,* she relied on how things were when her son and his friends Danny and Doug, Ricky and Justin and Jim, were growing up.

Now she wishes she had kept a journal back in the days when she was growing up herself. She hopes *Jake's Journal* will encourage young people today to keep their own journals.